Thomas William Parsons

The Shadow of the Obelisk

And other Poems

Thomas William Parsons

The Shadow of the Obelisk
And other Poems

ISBN/EAN: 9783744765695

Printed in Europe, USA, Canada, Australia, Japan

Cover: Foto ©Andreas Hilbeck / pixelio.de

More available books at **www.hansebooks.com**

THE

SHADOW OF THE OBELISK

AND

OTHER POEMS.

BY

THOMAS WILLIAM PARSONS.

LONDON:

HATCHARDS, PICCADILLY.

1872.

To the Memory

OF

MY BEST AND EARLIEST FRIEND

DANIEL TREADWELL,

OF CAMBRIDGE, MASSACHUSETTS,

LATE RUMFORD PROFESSOR IN HARVARD COLLEGE.

CONTENTS.

THE SHADOW OF THE OBELISK.

—— combien d'hommes ont regardé cette ombre
en Egypte et à Rome?   CHATEAUBRIAND.

HOMEWARD turning from the music which had
　　wildered so my brain,
That my way I scarce remembered to the Quirinal
　　again,—
Not unwilling to forget it underneath a moon so fair,
In a solitude so sacred, and so summer-like an air,—
By the shore, I came, of Tiber, little conscious where I
　　stood,
Till I marked the yellow trembling of the light upon the
　　flood.

Tethered near, some broken barges hid the wave's august
　　repose ;
Petty sheds of humble dealers nigh the Campus Martius
　　rose ;
Hardly could the dingy Thamis, when his tide is ebbing
　　low,
Life's dull scene in colder colours to the homesick exile
　　show.

B

Winding from the vulgar prospect, through a labyrinth of
    lanes,
Forth I stood upon the Corso where its greatness Rome
    retains.

Yet it was not ancient glory, though the midnight radiance
    fell
Soft on many a princely mansion, many a dome's majestic
    swell;
Though, from some hushed corner gushing, oft a modern
    fountain gleamed,
Where the marble and the waters in their freshness equal
    seemed:
What though open courts unfolded columns of Corinthian
    mould?
Beautiful it was,—but altered! naught bespake the Rome
    of old.

So, regardless of the grandeur, passed I towards the
    Northern Gate;
All around were shining gardens,—churches glittering,
    yet sedate;
Heavenly bright the broad enclosure! but the o'erwhelm-
    ing silence brought
Stillness to mine own heart's beating, with a moment's
    turn of thought,
And it startled me to notice I was walking unaware,
O'er the Obelisk's tall shadow on the pavement of the square.

Ghost-like seemed it to address me, and conveyed me
 for a while,
Backward, through a thousand ages, to the borders of the
 Nile ;
Where the centuries watched its creeping from the morn
 when it begun,
O'er the stones perchance of Memphis, or the City of
 the Sun.
Kingly turrets looked upon it,—pyramids and sculptured
 fanes ;
Now the sand is king o'er Pharaoh, but the shadow still
 remains.

Out of Egypt came the trophy, from old empire to the
 new ;
Here the eternal apparition met the millions' daily view.
Virgil's foot has touched it often,—it hath kissed Octavia's
 face—
Royal chariots have rolled o'er it, in the frenzy of the
 race,
When the strong, the swift, the valiant, mid the thronged
 arena strove,
In the days of good Augustus, and the dynasty of Jove.

Herds are feeding in the Forum, as in old Evander's
 time ;
Tumbled from the steep Tarpeian all the towers that
 sprang sublime.

Strange! that what seemed most inconstant should the
    most abiding prove;
Strange! that what is hourly moving no mutation can
    remove;
Ruined lies the cirque! the chariots, long ago, have
    ceased to roll—
Even the Obelisk is broken,—but the shadow still is
    whole.

What is Fame! if mightiest empires leave so little mark
    behind,
How much less must heroes hope for, in the wreck of
    humankind!
Less than even this darksome picture, which I tread
    beneath my feet,
Copied by a lifeless moonbeam on the pebbles of the
    street:
Read the name upon the base there,—most of all Rome's
    names renowned,
Cæsar!—what left he behind him, save the shadow of a
    sound?

DECEMBER FOURTEENTH.*

Anniversary of the Death of Prince Albert, 1861.

A GLOOM of sickness, gathering in the East,
    Spreads over England growing to despair :
Outside the Prince's chamber waits a priest,
    With that last medicine for our clay, a prayer.

                 * *Calcutta, Dec.* 20, 1871.

'All sorts and conditions of men' in this great Empire—Jews, Hindoos, Mahommedans, Parsees, &c., as well as the different denominations of Christians—have, during the past fortnight, offered up prayers for the recovery of the Prince of Wales. On the 14th day of this month (a great Mahommedan festival—the ' Eeed-al-Ramzan ') a thousand Suni Mahommedans of all castes assembled for prayer in the great Mosque endowed by the sect at Bombay, and a leading member of the Suni Khoja Mahommedans prayed the Almighty for the recovery of the Prince. The day is said to have been selected as a peculiarly holy one, and the prayers to have been most fervent. A Mahommedan prayer-meeting will sound oddly to some good people in England, but it cannot fail to be pleasing to the Queen and the Royal Family to know that from men of all creeds in this great part of Her Majesty's dominions there has arisen one common and, I am sure, sincere prayer to the Great Father of all, entreating Him to spare the Heir to England's Throne.'—*Letter in the London ' Times.'*

Not now in state, a royal mother knelt,
  Thinking of this day ten dead years ago :
Last night the staghound wailed :—perchance it felt
  The sense those creatures have of coming woe.

Then England prayed : but not alone the isle
  Where England's throne is : on far Western plains
Beyond the seas men prayed, and in strange style
  Those dark-eyed Persians * in their Hindu fanes.

Then Alexandra, in her secret soul
  And silent closet, all alone with One
Who lent her of His own sweet self-control,
  Prayed to the Father, imaged in that Son :

' Let not the heir of England, O my God !
  Go to the grave without a story meet
  For such nobility of soul and birth ;
But in that high path which his father trod,
  Let him walk ever with unswerving feet,
  Until his reign accomplished be on earth.
Thou who art King of kings and all mankind,
  Who holdest in Thy hand the hearts of kings,
  Knowing their purposes and men's desire,
Be to my prayer Thy gracious ear inclined,
  In this December's darkest hour that brings
  Remembrance back of my lord's goodly sire,

        * The Parsees, or fire-worshippers.

Who went to glory with his crown of grace
   And spotless record in his princely hand,
   And all the kingdom sorrowing at his bier,
That Thou, who ever didst befriend his race,
   Wilt spare my husband for this weeping land,
   To serve it ever, as Thy servant here.'

Oh, Albert Edward! let the people say,
   In thee we know our Heaven-appointed king,
Because when all were heart-sick with dismay
   Hope fanned our fever with her constant wing;

And when the star of life was hardly seen
   Under one awful shadow in the storm,
That cloud was broken! and the blue serene
   Smiled,—and the star burned steadily and warm,

For England's prayer was heard by Him who made
   England so mighty! rich and free and strong.
O may that sceptre still be wisely swayed
   Which Heaven hath blest so largely and so long!

THE LAST GENTIAN.

SEE! I survive because I bowed my head,
　　Hearing the Snow's first footfall in the air;
I felt his cold kiss on my cheek with dread,
　　And to my sister said, Beware!
And stooped beneath my bank and let him pass.
Next morn the brook was glass:
My simple sister, in her pride,
Disdained to bow her head, so drooped and died.

Last gentian of the withering year!
　　Left for Augusta's hand,
Thou shalt not linger shivering here
　　By the bleak north wind fannéd,
Until thy blue eye turn to gray,
And from thy lids the lashes fall away.
I will not leave thee, loving thee so well,
　　To face the ruin of November's air;
But thou shalt go where Summer still doth dwell,
　　Soft light and bird-song,—all things bright or fair,—
And happy thoughts and wise thoughts fed with books,

And gentle speech, and loving looks
  From eyes that still make sunshine everywhere.
For know, thou trembling stem, that not alone
  My lady bears the summer in her name ;
Her heart is of that season ; and her tone
  When she shall greet thee,—guessing whence it came,—
And the sweet welcome of her smile
Thy simple soul shall so beguile,
That hadst thou lips as lids, those lips would say
The day I found thee was thy sunniest day.

Nov. 12.

GUIDO'S AURORA.

In the Rospigliosi Palace, Rome.

' La concubina di Titone antico
Già s' imbiancava al balzo d' oriente,
Fuor delle braccia del suo dolce amico :
Di gemme la sua fronte era lucente.'
— PURGATORIO, IX.

FORTH from the arms of her beloved now,
Whitening the Orient steep, the Concubine
Of old Tithonus comes, her lucent brow
Glistening with gems, her fair hands filled with flowers,
That drop their violet odours on the brine,
While from her girdle pours a wealth of pearls
Round ocean's rocks and every vessel's prow
That cuts the laughing billow's crested curls.
Behind her step the busy, sober Hours,
With much to do ;—and they must move apace :
Wake up, Apollo! should the women stir,
And thou be lagging? brighten up thy face!
(Those eyes of Phaeton more brilliant were)
Hurry, dull God! Hyperion, to thy race!

Thy steeds are galloping, but thou seem'st slow :
  Hesper, glad wretch, hath newly fed his torch,
And flies before thee, and the world cries, Go!
  Light the dark woods, the dew-drenched mountain
    scorch!
Phœbus, Aurora calls, why linger so?

TO HENRY WADSWORTH LONGFELLOW.

THINK not that this enchanted isle
    Wherein I dwell, some days a king,
Postpones till June its tardy smile,
    And only knows imagined spring.

Not yet my lilies are in bloom ;
    But lo ! my cherry, bridal-white,
Whose sweetness fills my sunny room,
    The bees, and me, with one delight.

And on the brink of Lanham Brook
    The laughing cowslips catch mine eye,
As on the bridge I stop to look
    At the stray blossoms loitering by.

Our almond-willow waves its plumes
    In contrast with the dark-haired pine,
And in the morning sun perfumes
    The lane almost like summer's vine.

Dear Poet ! shouldst thou tread with me,
　Even in the spring, these woodland ways,
Under thy foot the violet see,
　And overhead the maple sprays,

Thou mightst forego thy Charles's claim,
　To wander by *our* stream awhile : 　·
So should these meadows grow to fame,
　And all the Muses haunt our Isle.

WAYLAND, MASSACHUSETTS.

FROM LONDON TO MILTON HILL.

THE wounded man, fresh from the bitter field
    · And the rough ambulance,—dear lady mine !
In dreadful hospitals, outstretched in pain,—
When the soft ministry of woman's hand
Wipes from his waxen brow the blood congealed
(That paints the peril where he had to stand)
And pours the comfort of her oil and wine
Until he opens his dead eyes again,
And looks the blessing that he cannot speak,—
Feels as I felt when those delightful words
Brought me back wandering in delirium wild
(My brain all fever and my whole frame weak)
To sense again.   Methought I was a child,
Listening in meadows to Spring's welcome birds,
And, for the first time in a month, I smiled.

O my sweet lady, noblest of the fair,
And fairest among noblesse,—write again !
Gifts like thine own must always be to spare ;
God, when He giveth, *amply* gives to men :
Could borrowing make *thy* heart's abundance bare ?

23 PALL MALL, *January*, 1872.

LETTER FROM AMERICA TO A FRIEND
IN TUSCANY.

ON the rough Bracco's top, at break of day,
    High o'er that gulf which bounds the Genoese,
Since thou and I pursued our mountain way,
    Twenty Decembers have disrobed the trees.

Charmed by the glowing earth and golden sky,
    In Arno's vale you made yourself a nest;
There perched in peace and bookish ease, while I,
    In love with Freedom, sought her in the West.

And here, amid remembrances that throng
    Thicker than blossoms in the new-born June,
Thine chiefly claims the token of a song
    That still, at least, my heart remains in tune.

But who can sing amid this roar of streets,
    This crash of engines and discordant mills,
Where even in Solitude's most lone retreats
    Some factory drowns the music of the rills?

True, Nature here hath donned her gala robe,
    Rich in all charms,—bland, savage, and sublime ;
Within one realm enfolding half the globe,
    Flowers of all soils, and fruits of every clime.

But yet no bard, with consecrating touch,
    Hath made the scene a nobler mood inspire ;
The sullen Puritan, the sensual Dutch,
    Proved but a barren fosterage for the lyre.

Here, by the ploughman, as with daily tread
    He tracks the furrows of his virgin ground,
Dark locks of hair, and thigh-bones of the dead,
    Spear-heads, and skulls, and arrow-heads are found.

On such memorials unconcerned we gaze ;
    No trace returning of the glow divine,
Wherewith, dear WALTER ! in our Eton days
    We eyed a fragment from the Palatine.

Cellini's workmanship could nothing add,
    Nor the Pope's blessing, nor a case of gold,
To the strange value every pebble had
    O'er which perhaps the Tiber's wave had rolled.

A like enchantment all thy land pervades,
    Mellows the sunshine, softens Autumn's breeze,
O'erhangs the mouldering town, and chestnut shades,
    And glows and sparkles in her storied seas.

No such a spell the charmed adventurer guides
    Who seeks those ruins hid in Yucatan,
Where through the tropic forest, silent, glides,
    By crumbled fane and idol, slow Copàn.

There, as the weedy pyramid he climbs,
    Or views, mid groves that rankly wave above,
The work of nameless hands in unknown times,
    Much wakes his wonder—nothing stirs his love.

Art's rude beginnings, wheresoever found,
    The same dull chord of feeling faintly strike ;
The Druid's pillar, and the Indian mound,
    And Uxmal's monuments, are mute alike.

And here, although the gorgeous year hath brought
    Crimson October's beautiful decay,
Seldom this loveliness inspires a thought
    Beyond the marvels of the fleeting day.

For here the Present overpowers the Past ;
    No recollections to these woods belong,
O'er which no minstrelsy its veil hath cast,
    To rouse our worship, or supply my song.

But these will come ; the necromancer Age
    Shall round the wilderness his glory throw ;
Hudson shall murmur through the poet's page,
    And in his numbers more superbly flow.

                          c

Enough,—'tis more than midnight by the clock;
   Manhattan dreams of dollars, all abed:
With you, dear Walter, 'tis the crow of cock,
   And o'er Fièsole the skies are red.

Good-night! yet stay—both longitudes to suit,
   Your own returning, and my absent light,
Thus let me bid our mutual salute;
   To you *buon giorno*—for myself good-night!

THE WILLEY HOUSE.

A Ballad of the White Hills.

I.

COME, children put your baskets down,
    And let the blushing berries be ;
Sit here and wreathe a laurel crown,
    And if I win it, give it me.

'Tis afternoon,—it is July,—
    The mountain shadows grow and grow ;
Your time of rest, and mine is nigh—
    The moon was rising long ago.

While yet on old Chocŏrua's top
    The lingering sunlight says farewell,
Your purple-fingered labour stop,
    And hear a tale I have to tell.

II.

You see that cottage in the glen,
    Yon desolate, forsaken shed,
Whose mouldering threshold now and then
    Only a few stray travellers tread.

No smoke is curling from its roof,
   At eve no cattle gather round,
No neighbour now, with dint of hoof,
   Prints his glad visit on the ground.

A happy home it was of yore :
   At morn the flocks went nibbling by,
And Farmer Willey, at his door,
   Oft made their reckoning with his eye.

Where yon rank alder-trees have sprung,
   And birches cluster, thick and tall,
Once the stout apple overhung,
   With his red gifts, the orchard wall.

Right fond and pleasant in their ways
   The gentle Willey people were ;
I knew them in those peaceful days,
   And Mary,—every one knew her.

III.

Two summers now had seared the hills,
   Two years of little rain or dew ;
High up the courses of the rills
   The wild-rose and the raspberry grew :

The mountain sides were cracked and dry,
   And frequent fissures on the plain,
Like mouths, gaped open to the sky
   As though the parched earth prayed for rain.

One sultry August afternoon,
   Old Willey, looking toward the West,
Said—'We shall hear the thunder soon :
   Oh ! if it bring us rain, 'tis blest.'

And even with his word, a smell
   Of sprinkled fields passed through the air,
And from a single cloud there fell
   A few large drops,—the rain was there.

Ere set of sun a thunder-stroke
   Gave signal to the floods to rise :
Then the great seal of heaven was broke,
   Then burst the gates that barred the skies !

While from the West the clouds rolled on,
   And from the Nor'west gathered fast ;
' We'll have enough of rain anon,'
   Said Willey,—' if this deluge last.'

For all these cliffs that stand sublime
   Around, like solemn priests appeared,
Gray druids of the olden time,
   Each with his white and streaming beard.

Till in one sheet of seething foam
   The mingling torrents joined their might ;
But in the Willeys' quiet home
   Was naught but silence and ' Good-night !'

For soon they went to their repose,
  And in their beds, all safe and warm,
Saw not how fast the waters rose,
  Heard not the growing of the storm.

But just before the stroke of ten,
  Old Willey looked into the night,
And called upon his two hired men,
  And woke his wife, who struck a light;

Though her hand trembled, as she heard
  The horses whinnying in the stall,
And—'Children!' was the only word,
  That woman from her lips let fall.

'Mother!' the frighted infants cried,
  'What is it? has a whirlwind come?'
Wildly the weeping mother eyed
  Each little darling, but was dumb.

A sound! as though a mighty gale
  Some forest from its hold had riven,
Mixed with a rattling noise like hail,
  God! art Thou raining rocks from heaven?

A flash! O Christ! the lightning showed
  The mountain moving from his seat!
Out! out into the slippery road!
  Into the wet with naked feet!

No time for dress,—for life ! for life !
   No time for any word but this :
The father grasped his boys,—his wife
   Snatched her young babe,—but not to kiss.

And Mary with the younger girl,
   Barefoot and shivering in their smocks,
Sped forth amid that angry whirl
   Of rushing waves and whelming rocks.

For down the mountain's crumbling side,
   Full half the mountain from on high
Came sinking, like the snows that slide
   From the great Alps about July.

And with it went the lordly ash,
   And with it went the kingly pine ;
Cedar and oak amid the crash,
   Dropped down like clippings of the vine.

Two rivers rushed,—the one that broke
   His wonted bounds and drowned the land,
And one that streamed with dust and smoke,
   A flood of earth, of stones and sand.

Then for a time the vale was dry,
   The soil had swallowed up the wave ;
Till one star looking from the sky,
   A signal to the tempest gave :

The clouds withdrew, the storm was o'er,
  Bright Aldebàran burned again;
The buried river rose once more,
  And foamed along his gravelly glen.

IV.

At morn the men of Conway felt
  Some dreadful thing had chanced that night,
And those by Breton woods who dwelt
  Observed the mountain's altered height.

Old Crawford and the Fabyan lad
  Came down from Amonoosuck then,
And passed the Notch,—ah! strange and sad
  It was to see the ravaged glen.

But having toiled for miles, in doubt,
  With many a risk of limb and neck,
They saw, and hailed with joyful shout
  The Willey House amid the wreck.

That avalanche of stones and sand,
  Remembering mercy in its wrath,
Had parted, and on either hand,
  Pursued the ruin of its path.

And there upon its pleasant slope,
  The cottage, like a sunny isle
That wakes the shipwrecked seaman's hope,
  Amid that horror seemed to smile.

And still upon the lawn before,
　　The peaceful sheep were nibbling nigh;
But Farmer Willey at his door
　　Stood not to count them with his eye.

And in the dwelling,— O despair!
　　The silent room! the vacant bed!
The children's little shoes were there—
　　But whither were the children fled?

That day a woman's head, all gashed,
　　Its long hair streaming in the flow,
Went o'er the dam, and then was dashed
　　Among the whirlpools down below.

And farther down, by Saco side,
　　They found the mangled forms of four,
Held in an eddy of the tide;
　　But Mary, she was seen no more.

Yet never to this mournful vale
　　Shall any maid, in Summer time,
Come without thinking of the tale
　　I now have told you, in my rhyme.

And when the Willey House is gone,
　　And its last rafter is decayed,
Its history may yet live on
　　In this your ballad that I made.

ON THE DEATH OF DANIEL WEBSTER.

Twenty-fourth of October, 1852.

COMES there a frigate home? what mighty bark
   Returns with torn, but still triumphant sails?
Such peals awake the wondering Sabbath,— hark!
   How the dread echoes die among the vales!

What ails the morning, that the misty sun
   Looks wan and troubled in the Autumn air?
Dark over Marshfield!—'twas the minute gun:
   God! has it come that we foreboded there?

The woods at midnight heard an angel's tread;
   The sere leaves rustled in his withering breath;
The night was beautiful with stars; we said,
   'This is the harvest moon,'—'twas thine, O Death!

Gone, then, the splendour of October's day!
   A single night, without the aid of frost,
Has turned the gold and crimson into gray,
   And the world's glory, with our own, is lost.

A little while, and we rode forth to greet
   His coming with glad music, and his eye
Drew many captives, as along the street
   His peaceful triumph passed, unquestioned, by.

Now there are moanings, by the desolate shore,
   That are not ocean's; by the patriot's bed,
Hearts throb for him whose noble heart no more—

Break off the rhyme,—for sorrow cannot stop
   To trim itself with phrases for the ear,—
Too fast the tears upon the paper drop:

Fast as the leaves are falling on his bier,
   Thick as the hopes that clustered round his name,
While yet he walked with us, a pilgrim here.

He was our prophet, our majestic oak,
   That, like Dodona's, in Thesprotian land,
Whose leaves were oracles, divinely spoke.

We called him giant, for in every part
   He seemed colossal; in his port and speech,
In his large brain and in his larger heart.

And when his name upon the roll we saw
   Of those who govern, then we felt secure,
Because we knew his reverence for the law.

So the young master* of the Roman realm
　　Discreetly thought, we cannot wander far
From the true course with Ulpian at the helm.

But slowly to this loss our sense awakes;
　　To know what space it in the forum filled,
See what a gap the temple's ruin makes!

Kings have their dynasties, but not the mind;
　　Cæsar leaves other Cæsars to succeed,
But Wisdom, dying, leaves no heir behind.

Who now shall stand the regent at the wheel?
　　Who knows the dread machinery? who hath skill
Our course through oceans unsurveyed to feel?

Her mournful tidings Albion lately sent,
　　How he, the victor in so many fields,
Fell, but not fighting, in the fields of Kent;

The chief whose conduct in the lofty scene
　　Where England stood up for the world in arms,
Gave her victorious name to England's queen.

But peaceful Britain knows, amid her grief
　　She could spare now the soldier and his sword;
What can our councils do without our chief?

　　　　　* Alexander Severus.

Blest are the peace-makers!—and he was ours,
　　Winning, by force of argument, the right
Between two kindred, more than rival powers.

Resume the rhyme, and end the funeral strain ;
　　Dying, he asked for song,—he did not slight
The harmony of numbers,— let the main
　　Sing round his grave great anthems, day and night.

The Autumn rains are falling on his head,
　　The snows of Winter soon will shroud the shore,
The Spring with violets will adorn his bed,
　　And Summer shall return,—but he, no more !

We have no high cathedral for his rest,
　　Dim with proud banners and the dust of years ;
All we can give him is New England's breast
　　To lay his head on,—and his country's tears.

NOVEMBER IST, 1852.

HUDSON RIVER.

RIVERS that roll most musical in song
    Are often lovely to the mind alone ;
The wanderer muses, as he moves along
    Their vacant banks, on glories not their own.

When, to give substance to his boyhood's dreams,
    He leaves his land, far countries to survey,
Oft must he think, in greeting foreign streams,
    ' Their names alone are beautiful, not they.'

If chance he mark the dwindled Arno pour
    A tide more meagre than his native Charles ;
Or views the Rhone when summer's heat is o'er,
    Subdued and stagnant in the fen of Arles ;

Or when he sees the slimy Tiber fling
    His sullen tribute at the feet of Rome,
Oft to his thought must partial memory bring
    More noble waves, without renown, at home ;

Now let him climb the Catskill, to behold
    The lordly Hudson, marching to the main,
And say what bard, in any land of old,
    Had such a river to inspire his strain.

Along the Rhine, gray battlements and towers
    Declare what robbers once the realm possessed;
But here Heaven's handiwork surpasseth ours,
    And man has hardly more than built his nest.

No storied castle overawes these heights,
    Nor antique arches check the current's play,
No mouldering architrave the mind invites
    To dream of deities long passed away.

But cliffs, unaltered from their primal form
    Since the subsiding of the deluge, rise
Above the lightnings of the midway storm,
    While far below the skiff securely plies.

And these deep woods forever have remained
    Touched by no axe,—by no proud owner nursed:
As now they look they looked when Pharaoh reigned,
    Lineal descendants of creation's first.

Thou Scottish Tweed, a sacred streamlet now !*
    Since thy last minstrel laid him down to die,
Where through the casement of his chamber thou
    Didst mix thy moan with his departing sigh ;

* 'As I was dressing, on the morning of Monday, the 17th of
September, Nicolson came into my room, and told me that his
master had awoke in a state of composure and consciousness, and
wished to see me immediately. I found him entirely himself,
though in the last extreme of feebleness. His eye was clear and
calm ;—every trace of the wild fire of delirium extinguished.

A single stretch of Hudson's ampler hills
  Might furnish forests for the whole of thine,
Hide in thick shade all Humber's feeding rills,
  And darken all the fountains of the Tyne.

Imperial Thames !—could all his riches buy,
  To gild the strand which London loads with gold,
Sunshine so bright,—such purity of sky
  As bless thy sultry season and thy cold ?

No tales, we know, are chronicled of thee
  In ancient scrolls ; no deeds of doubtful claim
Have hung a history on every tree,
  And given each rock its fable and a fame.

" Lockhart," he said, " I may have but a minute to speak to you.
My dear, be a good man ;—be virtuous,— be religious,— be a good
man. Nothing else will give you any comfort when you come to
lie here." He paused, and I said, " Shall I send for Sophia and
Anne ?"—" No," said he ; " don't disturb them. Poor souls !
I know they were up all night. God bless you all !" With this
he sunk into a very tranquil sleep, and, indeed, he scarcely after-
wards gave any sign of consciousness, except for an instant on the
arrival of his sons. They, on learning that the scene was about to
close, obtained a new leave of absence from their posts ; and both
reached Abbotsford on the 19th. About half-past one P.M., on
the 21st of September, Sir Walter breathed his last, in the presence of all his children. It was a beautiful day,—so warm that
every window was wide open, and so perfectly still that the sound of
all others most delicious to his ear—the gentle ripple of the Tweed
over its pebbles—was distinctly audible, as we knelt around the bed;
and his eldest son kissed and closed his eyes.'—LOCKHART'S LIFE
OF SIR WALTER SCOTT.

But neither here hath any conqueror trod,
　Nor grim invader from barbarian climes ;
No horrors feigned of giant or of god
　Pollute thy stillness with recorded crimes.

Here never yet have happy fields laid waste,
　The ravished harvest and the blasted fruit,
The cottage ruined, and the shrine defaced,
　Tracked the foul passage of the feudal brute.

' Yet, O Antiquity !' the stranger sighs,
　' Scenes wanting thee soon pall upon the view ;
The soul's indifference dulls the sated eyes,
　Where all is fair indeed,—but all is new.'

False thought ! is age to crumbling walls confined ?
　To Grecian fragments and Egyptian bones ?
Hath Time no monuments to raise the mind,
　More than old fortresses and sculptured stones ?

Call not this new which is the only land
　That wears unchanged the same primeval face
Which, when just dawning from its Maker's hand,
　Gladdened the first great grandsire of our race.

Nor did Euphrates with an earlier birth
　Glide past green Eden towards the unknown south,
Than Hudson broke upon the infant earth,
　And kissed the ocean with his nameless mouth.

Twin-born with Jordan, Ganges, and the Nile !
   Thebes and the Pyramids to thee are young ;
Oh ! had thy waters burst from Britain's isle,
   Till now perchance they had not flowed unsung.

ON A MAGNOLIA FLOWER.

MEMORIAL of my former days!
 Magnolia, as I scent thy breath,
And on thy pallid beauty gaze,
 I feel not far from death.

So much hath happened! and so much
 The tomb hath claimed of what was mine!
Thy fragrance moves me with a touch
 As from a hand divine:

So many dead! so many wed!
 Since first, by this Magnolia's tree,
I pressed a gentle hand, and said
 A word no more for me!

Lady, who sendest from the South
 This frail, pale token of the past,
I press the petals to my mouth,
 And sigh,—as 'twere my last.

Oh, love, we live, but many fell!
 The world's a wreck, but we survive!
Say, rather, still on earth we dwell,
 But gray at thirty-five!

STEUART'S BURIAL.

THE bier is ready and the mourners wait,
　　The funeral car stands open at the gate.
Bring down our brother; bear him gently, too;
So, friends, he always bore himself with you.
Down the sad staircase, from the darkened room,
For the first time, he comes in silent gloom :
Who ever left this hospitable door
Without his smile and warm 'good-bye,' before?
Now we for him the parting word must say
To the mute threshold whence we bear his clay.

The slow procession lags upon the road,—
'Tis heavy hearts that make the heavy load ;
And all too brightly glares the burning noon
On the dark pageant,—be it ended soon !
The quail is piping and the locust sings,—
O grief, thy contrast with these joyful things !
What pain to see, amid our task of woe,
The laughing river keeps its wonted flow !

His hawthorns there, his proudly-waving corn,
And all so flourishing,—and so forlorn!
His new-built cottage, too, so fairly planned,
Whose chimney ne'er shall smoke at his command.

Two sounds were heard, that on the spirit fell
With sternest moral,—one the passing bell!
The other told the history of the hour,
Life's fleeting triumph, mortal pride and power.
Two trains there met,—the iron-sinewed horse
And the black hearse,—the engine and the corse!
Haste on your track, you fiery-wingèd steed!
I hate your presence and approve your speed;
Fly! with your eager freight of breathing men,
And leave these mourners to their march again!
Swift as my wish, they broke their slight delay,
And Life and Death pursued their separate way.

The solemn service in the church was held,
Bringing strange comfort as the anthem swelled,
And back we bore him to his long repose,
Where his great elm its evening shadow throws,—
A sacred spot! There often he hath stood,
Showed us his harvests and pronounced them good;
And we may stand, with eyes no longer dim,
To watch new harvests and remember him.

Peace to thee, STEUART!—and to us! the All-Wise
Would ne'er have found thee readier for the skies:

In His large love He kindly waits the best,
The fittest mood, to summon every guest ;
So, in his prime, our dear companion went,
When the young soul is easy to repent :
No long purgation shall he now require
In black remorse,—in penitential fire ;
From what few frailties might have stained his morn
Our tears may wash him pure as he was born.

Epitaph upon my Friend, David Steuart Robertson.

From his grave-stone at Lancaster.

Here STEUART sleeps : and should some brother Scot
Wander this way, and pause upon the spot,
He need not ask, now life's poor show is o'er,
What arms he carried, or what plaid he wore :
So small the value of illustrious birth,
Brought to this solemn, last assay of earth !
Yet, unreproved, his epitaph might say
A royal soul was wrapt in STEUART'S clay,
And generous actions consecrate his mound,
More than all titles, though of kingly sound.

CAMPANILE DI PISA.

SNOW was glistening on the mountains, but the air
was that of June,
Leaves were falling, but the runnels playing still their
Summer tune,
And the dial's lazy shadow hovered nigh the brink of
noon.
On the benches in the market rows of languid idlers lay,
When to Pisa's nodding belfry, with a friend, I took
my way.

From the top we looked around us, and as far as eye
might strain,
Saw no sign of life or motion, in the town, or on the
plain;
Hardly seemed the river moving, through the willows to
the main;
Nor was any noise disturbing Pisa from her drowsy
hour,
Save the doves that fluttered 'neath us, in and out, and
round the tower.

Not a shout from gladsome children, nor the clatter of a
    wheel,
Nor the spinner of the suburb winding his discordant reel,
Nor the stroke upon the pavement of a hoof or of a
    heel :
Even the slumberers, in the churchyard of the Campo
    Santo, seemed
Scarce more quiet than the living world that underneath
    us dreamed.

Dozing at the city's portal, heedless guard the sentry
    kept,
More than Oriental dulness o'er the sunny farms had
    crept,
Near the walls the ducal herdsman by the dusty road-
    side slept ;
While his camels,* resting round him, half alarmed the
    sullen ox,
Seeing those Arabian monsters pasturing with Etruria's
    flocks.

---

* Near Pisa, a herd of camels is kept, upon a farm belonging to
the Grand Duke. The ancestors of these animals were brought
thither during the Crusades. Some of them are employed in the
work of the farm, and others may be met straying about in the
pine-woods or along the sands of the coast.

'These sands, with the sea, the camels, the purity and brightness
of the sky, the solitude and silence, give this picture something
Oriental, novel, and poetical, which pleases the fancy, and transports
it to the desert.'—VALERY.

Then it was, like one who wandered, lately, singing by
the Rhine,
Strains* perchance to maiden's hearing sweeter than
this verse of mine,
That we bade Imagination lift us on her wing divine.
And the days of Pisa's greatness rose from the sepulchral
past,
When a thousand conquering galleys bore her standard
at the mast.

Memory for a moment crowned her sovereign mistress of
the seas,
When she braved, upon the billows, Venice and the
Genoese,
Daring to deride the Pontiff, though he shook his angry
keys ;
When her admirals triumphant, riding o'er the Soldan's
waves,
Brought from Calvary's holy mountain fitting soil for
knightly graves.

When the Saracen surrendered, one by one, his pirate
isles,
And Ionia's marble trophies decked Lungarno's Gothic
piles,
Where the festal music floated in the light of ladies'
smiles ;

* The Belfry of Bruges.

Soldiers in the busy court-yard, nobles in the halls
    above —
Oh! those days of arms are over—arms and courtesy and
    love!

Now, as on Achilles' buckler, next a peaceful scene
    succeeds ;
Pious crowds in the cathedral duly tell their blessed
    beads ;
Students walk the learned cloister,—Ariosto wakes the
    reeds —
Science dawns,—and Galileo opens to the Italian youth,
As he were a new Columbus, new-discovered realms of
    truth.

Hark! what murmurs from the million in the bustling
    market rise !
All the lanes are loud with voices, all the windows dark
    with eyes ;
Black with men the marble bridges, heaped the shores
    with merchandise ;
Turks and Greeks and Libyan merchants in the square
    their councils hold,
And the Christian altars glitter, gorgeous with Byzantine
    gold !

Look! anon the masqueraders don their holiday attire;
Every palace is illumined,—all the town seems built of
    fire—

Rainbow-coloured lanterns dangle from the top of every
    spire :
Pisa's patron saint hath hallowed to himself the joyful
    day,
Never on the thronged Rialto showed the Carnival more
    gay.

Suddenly the bell beneath us broke the vision with its
    chime;
'Signors,' quoth our gray attendant, 'it is almost vesper
    time ;'
Vulgar life resumed its empire,—down we dropt from the
    sublime.
Here and there a friar passed us, as we paced the silent
    streets,
And a cardinal's rumbling carriage roused the sleepers
    from the seats.

THE ROSARY.

I FOUND a rosary at my feet,
 Amid the festive hall;
How beautiful! from Rome,—how sweet!—
 Devotion at a ball!

A cross, an amulet, a charm,
 Might 'stay the morning star!'
These pearls,—I wonder from whose arm,
 What angel's arm, they are.

I sought her out amid the crowd,
 With tresses largely laden;
Dark-eyed, but pale, a lofty-browed
 And Spanish-looking maiden.

'Lady, is't thine, this fair machine,
 This toy, faith's pretty fungus?
"Have we a Bourbon," then,—I mean
 A Romanist, among us?'

While thus the trinket I returned
  To her whose wrist adorned it,
Methought her cheek a moment burned,
  As though my speech had scorned it.

And, as she took the bauble back,
  A casual thought come o'er me :
This girl is on as good a track,
  Perchance, as hers who bore me.

She was a generous, discreet,
  And much-enduring mother,
Who early trained my little feet
  To kirkward with my brother.

Blest in belief, we did not know
  Of orthodox or Arian ;
Knew not if we were high or low,
  Baptist or Trinitarian.

We only knew that Christ was child
  Of God, and was our brother ;
That once on children He had smiled,
  And said, ' Love one another.'

God loved my brother more than me :
  The poor lame boy died early ;
While I grew up from croup to be
  Rough, tough, and tall and burly ;

And mixed with men, and wandered wide,
    And found that creeds were plenty;
And laughed at all, though I complied,
    As fashion taught, with twenty.

In France I worshipped Rochefoucault;
    In Italy, the singers,
And all the bearded tribe that owe
    Their fortune to their fingers.

In Germany they made me mad
    With their too much of learning
(Though less than he of Tarsus had),
    And blind with much discerning.

Our cousin-Germans were, for me,
    Not 'German to the matter :'
I heard their talk, but could not see
    Amid the smoke and clatter.

They reasoned in, and reasoned out,
    Yet gave me no assistance,
Until, at last, I came to doubt
    God's and my own existence.

And now I found me all astray,
    Begirt with shining errors,
.Wherewith philosophers of clay
    Outfaced the eternal terrors,

Since men of science, men of mind,
 Great reasoners, great scholars,
Taught me the sum of life to find
 In dinners, or in dollars.

' First good, first perfect, and first fair—'
 Youth's dreams, to end in eating !
Plato, we vainly wandered there,
 If all *thy* dreams were cheating.

Out of this dark, pedantic wood,
 This weary waste of paper ;
Out of this gloom to any good,
 Light, light, if but a taper.

And lo ! the Sun of Righteousness,
 All calm and clear before me ;
Thou Nazarene ! in my distress,
 Thy Word alone upbore me :

Back to my childhood's faith once more ;
 Back to my mother's lesson ;
Back to the cross that Jesus bore,
 His pardon and His blessing.

Lady, I do *not* scorn that sign,
 Howe'er our creeds depart :
Those beads,—that crucifix of thine—
 I kiss it,—in my heart.

'SOTTO L'USBERGO DEL SENTIRSI PURO.'

BRUSH not the floor where my lady hath trod,
  Lest one light sign of her foot you mar;
For where she hath walked, in the Spring, on the sod,
  There, I have noticed, most violets are.

Touch not her work, nor her book, nor a thing
  That her exquisite finger hath only pressed;
But fan the dust off with a plume that the wing
  Of a ring-dove let fall, on his way to his nest.

I think the sun stops, if a moment she stand,
  In the morn, sometimes, at her father's door;
And the brook where she may have dipt her hand
  Runs clearer to me than it did before.

Under the mail of 'I know me pure,'
  I dare to *dream* of her; and, by day,
As oft as I come to her presence, I'm sure
  Had I one low thought, she would look it away.

TO A LILAC.

I.

O LILAC, in whose purple well
   Youth *in perpetuo* doth dwell,
My fancy feels thy fragrant spell.

II.

Of all that morning dew-drops feed,
All flowers of garden, field, or mead,
Thou art the first in childhood's creed :

III.

And even to me thy breath, in spring,
Hath power, a little while, to bring
Back to my heart its blossoming.

IV.

I seem again, with pupil's pace,
And happy, shining, morning-face,
Bound school-ward, running learning's race.

E

V.

Thou, too, recall'st the tender time,
After my primer, ere my prime,
When love was born and life was rhyme ;

VI.

My morning ramble, all alone ;
My moonlit walk by haunted stone ;
My love, that ere it fledged was flown !

VII.

At noon, tired out with hateful task,
I fling aside my worldling's mask,
And for my bunch of lilac ask.

VIII.

At vesper-time, Celestial tea
Hath no refreshment like to thee,
Whose breath is nourishment for me.

IX.

At midnight, when my friends are gone,
And I sit down to ponder on
The day, what it hath lost or won,

X.

Thy perfume, like a flageolet
That once, by dark Bolsena's lake,
  What time the sun made golden set,
  I heard (and seem to hear it yet) !
A thousand memories doth awake

Of busy boyhood's vanished powers ;
  Of young ambition, flushed with praise ;
Of old companions, and of hours
  That had the sunshine of whole days ;
  Of Italy, and Roman ways ;
Of Tuscan ladies, courteous, fair,
And kind as beautiful,—forbear!
O Memory,—those impassioned eyes !
Beware ! for that way madness lies !

XI.

Sweet lilac, thou art come to June,
And all our orioles are in tune :
Thy doom is,—to be withering soon.

XII.

And so, farewell ! for other flowers
Must have their day; and mortal powers
Cannot love all things at all hours.

XIII.

Soon I shall have my *flower de luce*,
And the proud peony, whose use
It is to teach me pride's abuse.

XIV.

For proud am I as proud can be ;
But when that crimson gaud I see,
My lilac's memory comes to me,

WITH A VOLUME OF KEATS.

HIS name was writ in water.' Yes, too young
    The minstrel perished to have earned a name
To face the cold blight of the critic's tongue,
And his fresh laurels cankered ere they came.

Loved Adonàis? martyr to the boon
Which the gods gave, or promised, at his birth !
Think,—in lamenting that he died so soon,
How few such memories live so long on earth !

Full oft must obloquy precede renown :
Ere the saint's picture wear its ring of light
The living head must feel the thorny crown ;
The stars !—where were they, if there came no Night?

Know, love, the poet must not yield alone
Honey and roses,—fire must dwell within ;
The fairest flesh must underneath have bone,
The fiercest beast may wear the softest skin.

And something rough and resolute and sour
Must with the sweetness of the soul combine ;
For, although gentleness be part of power,
'Tis only strength makes gentleness divine.

BIRTH-PLACE OF ROBERT BURNS.

A LOWLY roof of simple thatch,—
  No home of pride, of pomp, and sin,—
So freely let us lift the latch,
  The willing latch that says, 'Come in.'

Plain dwelling this! a narrow door—
  No carpet by soft sandals trod,
But just for peasant's feet a floor,—
  Small kingdom for a child of God!

Yet here was Scotland's noblest born,
  And here Apollo chose to light;
And here those large eyes hailed the morn
  That had for beauty such a sight!

There, as the glorious infant lay,
  Some angel fanned him with his wing,
And whispered, ' Dawn upon the day
  Like a new sun! go forth and sing!'

He rose and sang, and Scotland heard—
  The round world echoed with his song,
And hearts in every land were stirred
  With love, and joy, and scorn of wrong.

Some their cold lips disdainful curled ;
   Yet the sweet lays would many learn ;
But he went singing through the world,
   In most melodious unconcern.

For flowers will grow, and showers will fall,
   And clouds will travel o'er the sky ;
And the great God, who cares for all,
   He will not let his darlings die.

But they shall sing in spite of men,
   In spite of poverty and shame,
And show the world the poet's pen
   May match the sword in winning fame.

ON A BUST OF DANTE.

SEE, from this counterfeit of him
    Whom Arno shall remember long,
How stern of lineament, how grim,
    The father was of Tuscan song:
There but the burning sense of wrong,
    Perpetual care and scorn, abide;
Small friendship for the lordly throng;
    Distrust of all the world beside.

Faithful if this wan image be,
    No dream his life was,—but a fight;
Could any Beatrìce see
    A lover in that anchorite?
To that cold Ghibeline's gloomy sight
    Who could have guessed the visions came
Of Beauty, veiled with heavenly light,
    In circles of eternal flame?

The lips as Cumæ's cavern close,
    The cheeks with fast and sorrow thin,

The rigid front, almost morose,
  But for the patient hope within,
Declare a life whose course hath been
  Unsullied still, though still severe,
Which, through the wavering days of sin,
  Kept itself icy-chaste and clear.

Not wholly such his haggard look
  When wandering once, forlorn, he strayed,
With no companion save his book,
  To Corvo's hushed monastic shade;
Where, as the Benedictine laid
  His palm upon the pilgrim guest,
The single boon for which he prayed
  The convent's charity was rest.*

Peace dwells not here,—this rugged face
  Betrays no spirit of repose;
The sullen warrior sole we trace,
  The marble man of many woes.
Such was his mien when first arose
  The thought of that strange tale divine,
When hell he peopled with his foes,
  The scourge of many a guilty line.

---

* It is told of DANTE that, when he was roaming over Italy, he
came to a certain monastery, where he was met by one of the friars,
who blessed him, and asked what was his desire; to which the
weary stranger simply answered, 'Pace.'

War to the last he waged with all
  The tyrant canker-worms of earth ;
Baron and duke, in hold and hall,
  Cursed the dark hour that gave him birth ;
He used Rome's harlot for his mirth ;
  Plucked bare hypocrisy and crime ;
But valiant souls of knightly worth
  Transmitted to the rolls of Time.

O Time ! whose verdicts mock our own,
  The only righteous judge art thou ;
That poor, old exile, sad and lone,
  Is Latium's other VIRGIL now :
Before his name the nations bow ;
  His words are parcel of mankind,
Deep in whose hearts, as on his brow,
  The marks have sunk of DANTE'S mind.

FRANCESCA DA RIMINI.

A Picture by Schoeffer.

YOU restless ghosts that roam the lurid air,
  I feel your misery,—for I was there;
Yea, not in dreams, but breathing and alive,
Have seen the storm, and heard the tempest drive :
Yet while the sleet went, withering as it past,
And the mad hail gave scourges to the blast,
While all was black below, and flame above,
Have thought,—'tis little to the storm of Love :
You know that sadly, know it to your cost,
Ah, too much loving, and for ever lost!

Still, suffering spirits, even your doom affords
Kisses and tears, however scant of words ;
Brief is your story, but it liveth long,—
Oh ! thank for that your poet and his song :
Be it some comfort, in that hateful Hell,
You had a lover of your love to tell ;

One that knew all,—the ecstasy, the gloom,
All the sad raptures that precede the tomb;
The fluttering hope, the triumph, and the care,—
The wild emotion, and the sure despair.

Not every friend hath friendship's finer touch,
To pardon passion, when it mounts too much;
Not every soul hath proved its own excess,
And feared the throb it still would not repress;
But he whose numbers gave you unto fame,
Lord of the lay,—I need not speak his name,—
Was one who felt; whose life was love or hate;
Born for extremes, he scorned the middle state;
And well he knew that, since the world began,
The heart was master in the world of man.

SONNET XIII.

From the Vita Nuova of Dante Alighieri.

S O gentle seems my lady and so pure
  When she greets any one, that scarce the eye
Such modesty and brightness can endure,
And the tongue, trembling, falters in reply.

She never heeds, when people praise her worth,—
Some in their speech, and many with a pen,
  But meekly moves, as if sent down to earth
To show another miracle to men !

  And such a pleasure from her presence grows
On him who gazeth, while she passeth by,—
  A sense of sweetness that no mortal knows
  Who hath not felt it,—that the soul's repose
  Is woke to worship, and a spirit flows
Forth from her face that seems to whisper, 'Sigh !'

TO JAMES RUSSELL LOWELL.

POET and friend! if any gift could bring
   A joy like that of listening while you sing,
'Twere such as this,—memorial of the days—
When Tuscan airs inspired more tender lays;
When the gray Apennine, or Lombard plain,
Sunburnt, or spongy with Autumnal rain,
Mingled perchance, as first they met your sight,
Some drops of disappointment with delight;
When, rudely wakened from the dream of years,
You heard Velino thundering in your ears,
And fancy drooped,—until Romagna's wine
Brought you new visions, thousand-fold more fine;
When first in Florence, hearkening to the flow
Of Arno's midnight music, hoarse below.
You thought of home, and recollected those
Who loved your verse, but hungered for your prose,
And more than all the sonnets that you made,
Longed for the letters,—ah, too poorly paid!
Thanks for thy boon! I look, and I am there;
The soaring belfry guides me to the square;

The punctual doves, that wait the stroke of one,
Flutter above me and becloud the sun;
'Tis Venice! Venice! and with joy I put
In Adria's wave, incredulous, my foot;
I smell the sea-weed, and again I hear
The click of oars, the screaming gondolier.
Ha! the Rialto,—Dominic! a boat;
Now in a gondola to dream and float:
Pull the slight cord and draw the silk aside,
And read the city's history as we glide;
For strangely here, where all is strange, indeed,
Not he who runs, but he who swims, may read.
Mark now, albeit the moral make thee sad,
What stately palaces these merchants had!
Proud houses once!—Grimani and Pisani,
Spinelli, Foscari, Giustiniani;
Behold their homes and monuments in one!
They writ their names in water, and are gone.
My voyage is ended, and all the round is past,—
See! the twin columns and the bannered mast,
The domes, the steeds, the Lion's wingèd sign,
' Peace to thee, Mark! Evangelist of mine!'*

Poetic art! reserved for prosy times
Of great inventions and of little rhymes;

* The legend of the winged Lion of Saint Mark, seen everywhere, at Venice—' Pax tibi, Marce! Evangelista meus.'

For us, to whom a wisely-ordering Heaven
Ether* for Lethe, wires for wings, has given
Whom vapours work for, yet who scorn a ghost,
Amid enchantments disenchanted most ;
Whose light, whose fire, whose messages had been
In blessed Urban's liberal days a sin,
Sure, in Damascus, any reasoning Turk
Would count your Talbotype a sorcerer's work.

Strange power ! that thus to actual presence brings
The shades of distant or departed things,
And calls dead Thebes or Athens up, or Arles,
To show like spectres on the banks of Charles !
But we receive this marvel with the rest ;
Nothing is new or wondrous in the West ;
Life's all a miracle, — and every age
To the great wonder-book but adds a page.

* Written just after the discovery in Boston, U.S., by Morton,
of the surgical use of ether.

TO A LADY,

In Return for a Book of Michel Angelo's Sonnets.

> 'Non ha l'ottimo artista alcun concetto
> Ch' un solo marmo in se non circoscriva
> Col suo soverchio,—e solo a quello arriva
> La man' che obbedisce all' intelletto.'
>
> *Sonnetto di Michel Angelo Buonarroti.*

NO master artist e'er imagines aught
    That lies not hid, awaiting mortal gaze,
In the rough marble,—if but fitly wrought
    By one whose hand his intellect obeys :
His magic touch the stone's white silence wakes,
And, lo ! the god from his long bondage breaks :

Breaks like the blue morn from an Orient vapour,
    Which made the pilgrim doubtful of the day ;
Or like the music from the written paper
    O'er which some poet lets his fancy play ;
Like new-born April from the Winter's tomb,
Or any joy that springs from any gloom.

Lady ! the fair material of our being
   Is put before us, to be carved at will :
Oh ! wisely work, with clear conception seeing
   The perfect shape that shall reward thy skill :
Something there may be, cut from every life,
Something to worship,—whether saint or wife.

Learn Patience first ; for Patience is the part
   Of all whom Time records among the great,
The only gift I know, the only art,
   To strengthen up our frailties to our fate :
Through long endurance comes the martyr crown
That makes the hero blush for his renown.

And, as by many steps, from thorn to flower,
   The patient petals of the rose recover
The hues and fragrance of the golden hour,
   That saw last Summer's nightingale her lover,
So may thy soul, if constancy be thine,
Toil on through trials till it dawn divine !

LOSS OF THE SHIP 'ARCTIC.'

THERE'S a gem in the goblet : Oh ! drink it, and say
If its taste be not salt as the wild ocean spray.
Is't a pearl or a chrysolite? tell—as I sip,
What gives it this bitter that palsies my lip ?

'Tis the gem in the goblet. Pause not ! Drink it down ;
'Twould outvalue the best in an emperor's crown;
'*Tis* a pearl, but it never was born in a shell :
Such a pearl from that mother at Calvary fell.

'Tis a crystal, but never was found in a mine !
'Tis a diamond ; but, ah, how it tastes of the brine !
Drink it down and have done, like the queen of the Nile :
Drink the pearl,—take the asp,— and be patient awhile.

Oh ! tell me the name of this treasure of thine,
What jewel it was that you dropt in the wine ;
What ruby or topaz, or what may it be
That makes the drink sparkle, and taste of the sea.

'Twas a thing that fell from me,—a tear that I shed
For the good and the lovely and brave that are dead.
I look up to the Day, but the fog hides the sun,
And the sky of October is mournful and dun.

I look to the Night, but Arcturus is there !
And the name of that vessel,* it gleams in the Bear :
I read it in all things, that story of woe !
In the stars o'er my head, and the waters below.

* Ἄρκτος.

UPON A LADY SINGING.

OFT as my lady sang for me
That song of the lost one that sleeps by the sea,
Of the grave and the rock, and the cypress tree,
Strange was the pleasure that over me stole,
For 'twas made of old sadness that lives in my soul.

So still grew my heart at each tender word,
That the pulse in my bosom scarcely stirred,
And I hardly breathed, but only heard:
Where was I?—not in the world of men,
Until she awoke me with silence again.

Like the smell of the vine, when its early bloom
Sprinkles the green lane with sunny perfume,
Such a delicate fragrance filled the room:
Whether it came from the vine without,
Or arose from her presence, I dwell in doubt.

Light shadows played on the pictured wall
From the maples that fluttered outside the hall,
And hindered the daylight,—yet, ah! not all;
Too little for that all the forest would be,—
Such a sunbeam she was to me!

When my sense returned, as the song was o'er,
I fain would have said to her, 'Sing it once more,'
But soon as she smiled my wish I forbore :
Music enough in her look I found,
And the hush of her lip seemed sweet as the sound.

SORRENTO.

M IDWAY betwixt the present and the past—
    Naples and Pæstum,—look! Sorrento lies :
Ulysses built it, and the Sirens cast
    Their spell upon the shore, the sea, the skies.

If thou hast dreamed, in any dream of thine,
    How Paradise appears, or those Elysian
Immortal meadows which the gods assign
    Unto the pure of heart,—behold thy vision!

These waters, they are blue beyond belief,
    And England's emerald meads are matched by these :
The sun,—'tis Italy's ; here winter's brief
    And gentle visit hardly chills the breeze.

Here Tasso dwelt, and here inhaled with Spring
    The breath of passion and the soul of song. ·
Here young Boccacio plumed his early wing,
    Thenceforth to soar above the vulgar throng,

All charms of contrast,—every nameless grace
    That lives in outline, harmony, or hue—
So heighten all the romance of the place,
    That the rapt artist maddens at the view,

And then despairs, and throws his pencil by,
   And sits all day and looks upon the shore
And the calm ocean with a languid eye,
   As though to labour were a law no more.

Voluptuous coast! no wonder that the proud
   Imperial Roman found in yonder isle
Some sunshine still to gild Fate's gathering cloud
   And lull the storm of conscience for a while.

What new Tiberius, tired of lust and life,
   May rest him here to give the world a truce,—
A little truce from perjury and strife,
   Justice adulterate and power's misuse?

Might the gross Bourbon,—he that sleeps in spite *
   Of red Vesuvius ever in his eye,
Yet, if he wake, should tremble at its light,
   As 'twere Heaven's vengeance, promised from on high,—

Might he, or any of Oppression's band,
   Sit here and learn the lesson of the scene,
Peace might return to many a bleeding land,
   And men grow just again, and life serene.

* Written at Naples, during the reign of the King that bombarded Palermo.

A SONG FOR SEPTEMBER.

SEPTEMBER strews the woodland o'er
  With many a brilliant colour;
The world is brighter than before —
  Why should our hearts be duller?
Sorrow and the scarlet leaf,
  Sad thoughts and sunny weather,
Ah me! this glory and this grief
  Agree not well together.

This is the parting season,—this
  The time when friends are flying;
And lovers now, with many a kiss,
  Their long farewells are sighing.
Why is earth so gaily drest?
  This pomp that Autumn beareth
A funeral seems, where every guest
  A bridal garment weareth.

Each one of us, perchance, may here,
  On some blue morn hereafter,
Return to view the gaudy year,
  But not with boyish laughter:

We shall then be wrinkled men,
Our brows with silver laden,
And thou this glen mayst seek again,
But nevermore a maiden !

Nature perhaps foresees that Spring
Will touch her teeming bosom,
And that a few brief months will bring
The bird, the bee, the blossom ;
Ah ! these forests do not know —
Or would less brightly wither—
The virgin that adorns them so
Will never more come hither !

VIVA LA MUSICA.

OUR House, that long in darkness dwelt,
    And long in silence, day by day,
Before the mountain snows could melt,
While yet the world was bleak and gray,
Received an impulse from the play
    Of sudden fingers on the strings,
That made the new-born meadows gay
    With magic touch, as 'twere the Spring's.

The melancholy frog no more
Shall pipe his burden, twanging shrill,
    The oriole gives his matins o'er,
No song-bird now hath any skill ;
Even that reproachful whip-poor-will *
    That stirred such memories in my heart,
Is hushed,—yet comes, a listener still,
    Nightly, to hear Cordelia's art.

O virgins of the silver lute !
O goddess of the golden chord !

* An American bird, so called from its note.

And thou great master of the flute,
Pan, of the reeds acknowledged lord !
Troop hither, and your best reward
    For your old music, in the days
When young Apollo was your king,
    Shall be to peep from yonder bays,
And hear your latest scholar sing.

GUY FAWKES DAY

At the Old House in Sudbury.

ONE fifth of November, when meadows were brown,
    And the crimson woods withered round Sudbury
        town,
Four lads from that city which Holmes calls the best,
At an old tavern met for a whole day of rest.

There was Henry and Austin and William and John,
And the glasses went round as the oak-wood went on,
And the spirit was kindly, the water was hot,—
Why then should Guy Fawkes and his day be forgot?

He was known in this tavern of old, I *expect*,
Though his name, like the turnpike, has come to neglect;
And I *guess* there was loyalty under this roof—
See! Her Majesty's picture remains for a proof.

But distinction is lost,—the Queen's nobody now,
And a sovereign is not worth a sixpence to Howe,
Though his fathers before him, the constant old carles,
By the name of their monarch did christen the Charles.

There be names on the window-panes written with rings,
When the gentles wore diamonds and all was the king's ;
When Joel and Hiram, as still they should do,
Served the punch, my dear Henry, to persons like you.

But the scutcheon is faded that hangs on the wall,
And the hearth looks forlorn in the desolate hall;
And the floor that has bent with the minuet's tread,
It is like a church-pavement,—the dancers are dead.

Yet we summoned them back, and recalled ancient times,
And we roused the old Papist, repeating his rhymes,
And, to help on the humour, each man, with his drink,
Gave the best match for Guido of whom he could think.

Well, we thought of all scandalous names that had been,
Cain, Catiline, Borgia,—the by-words of sin,
Saint Dominic Guzman,—Maràt,— Machiavèl,—
Though the splendour of that one we recognised well.

Then Austin propounded—a health to old Nol !
And those Roundheaded rogues whom our speakers extol:
And one mentioned Arnold, and one Aaron Burr,
And that Empress was named in the country of fur.

But we tired of such folk,—so to sweeten our toast,
Gave that noblest of bards Massachusetts can boast !
Famous now is this house in whose halls he hath been,
For his muse hath made sacred old Sudbury Inn !

THE OLD HOUSE IN SUDBURY TWENTY YEARS AFTERWARDS.*

'Our revels now are ended.'—*Tempest.*

THUNDER-CLOUDS may roll above him,
   And the bolt may rend his oak :
Lyman lieth where no longer
   He shall dread the lightning stroke.

Never to his father's hostel
   Comes a kinsman or a guest ;
Midnight calls for no more candles :
   House and landlord both have rest.

---

* This Old House is the one celebrated by Longfellow as the
Wayside Inn. It was the first large farmhouse and hostelry opened
on the highroad between Boston and the Connecticut River, and is
still occupied, though not as a tavern. It was always, from its erec-
tion in 1690, the estate of one family, whose last direct descendants
were Lyman Howe, and Adam his brother.

The former passed through life with a strange fear of lightning ;
but the dreaded stroke never came until many years after his death,
when the structure was somewhat damaged.

Adam's love and Adam's trouble
   Are a scarce-remembered tale;
No more wine-cups brightly bubble;
   No more healths, nor cakes, nor ale.

On the broken hearth, a dotard
   Sits, and fancies foolish things;
And the poet weaves romances,
   Which the maiden fondly sings,

All about the ancient hostel
   With its legends and its oaks;
And the quaint old-bachelor brothers,
   And their minstrelsy and jokes.

No man knows them any longer:
   All are gone, and I remain
Reading, as it were, mine epitaph
   On the rainbow-coloured pane.*

Blessings on them, dear initials!
   Henry W., Daniel T.,
E. and L. :— I'll not interpret;
   Let men wonder who they be.

Some are in their graves, and many
   Buried in their books and cares;

---

* Prismatic-hued from extreme age.

In the tropics, in Archangel:
Our thoughts are no longer theirs.

God have mercy;—all are sinful:—
Christ, conform our lives to Thine!
Keep us from all strife, ill-speaking,
Envy, and the curse of wine.

Fetch my steed; I cannot linger:
Buckley, quick; I must away:
Good old groom, take thou this nothing;
Millions could not make me stay.

THE SCALLOP-SHELL.

I CAME to the city that looks towards the sea,
But found on my table no scallop for me!
There were bills from the butcher, and billets from girls,
Things common as pebbles, and precious as pearls,
There were volumes of poetry, volumes of prose,—
By fifty new poets whom nobody knows;
There were things fair to look at, and things sweet to
    smell,
Engravings and nosegays,—but devil a shell!

Now, my lady, I teased her with many a prayer,
When she went to the ocean, to think of me there,
And to write me a letter at Sudbury Oaks,—
A page full of gossip, and all the best jokes!
This, indeed, she denied me,—but whispered, 'Write
    me,
And then I will think of you, down by the sea.'
'Oh, think of me *everywhere*, lady,—farewell!
But, to show that you think of me, send me a shell.'

Then I went to the greenwood,—I slept in the shade
Of the midsummer branches that sang serenade :
There I breathed the fresh meadows, I drank the warm
        vine,
I tasted the perfume that weeps from the pine,
And I lay by the brookside, a listening the bee,
And was lulled by the locust,—but thought of the sea ;
I picked the green apples by chance as they fell,
And I fed me with berries,—but sighed for my shell.

Back and forth to the wood with no song on my lips,
Back and forth to the city to gaze on the ships,—
To eye the tall vessels and smell of the sea,—
But scallop or cockle comes never to me !
I wander at daybreak, I sit late at night,—
And I think many things, but have no heart to write ;
No heart, dear, to speak of, 'tis mute in its cell,—
Could Apollo make music deprived of his shell ?

SUMMER-FLITTING.

I.

SAD Rosalind sits in the lonely hall;
  Silent as ever, she sits and sews,
Like a nun, for penance, at work on her pall,
Thinking the while on her sins and woes;
  She sighs, but sings not; for all are gone,—
  Ellen and Frances, Austin and John,—
  And silently her hand works on.

II.

Musing on many things—God above,
And life and death and the burning lake,
  And her work,—and everything but love,
For nothing her frozen heart can wake,—
  She stabs with her needle, but never sings;
  For oft in her ears a shrill bell rings,
  And she starts, as she heard an angel's wings.

III.

At nine o' the clock comes the Abbot in,
And whispers, ' Rosalind, what hast thou there ?'
  ' All day,' she answers, ' at work I have been
On a winding-sheet which I mean to wear,
  And now I am busy, hemming my pall ;
  For I heard, last night, the Death-Angel call,
  And the grass will soon grow over us all.'

IV.

At ten, Brother William came from his room,
Saying, ' Sister Rosalind, get thee to bed !'
  And he walked up and down, with a face of gloom,
More heavy of heart than he was in his tread ;
  For meagre he was, and worn in his looks,
  With hunting for sense in difficult nooks,
  .And words in hid corners of Latin books.

V.

Still, patient Rosalind never stirred,
But stitched away at the snow-white cloth,
  And answered the Brother never a word :
Whereat the sullen friar was wroth,
  And glided away, with his visage wan,
  Silent and sober ; for all were gone !—
  Brother Austin, and Brother John.

VI.

He met the cat in the corridor,
And the lean thing rubbed against his leg;
  So he lifted the creature from the floor,
Saying, 'Poor puss, thou need'st not beg;
  There's nothing,—nor milk, nor fowl, nor flesh,
Not a smelt from the hook, nor a quail from the mesh,—
  Nothing for thee, Tom, salt or fresh!

VII.

'Not even a puny mouse in the wall,
Nor a cup of cream on an upper shelf;
  For these roofs are abandoned by mice and all,
And I am as friendless as thyself;
  The chambers are empty,—the larder, too,—
  The grinders have ceased, they've grown so few,
  And there's no one to pray for but me and you!'

VIII.

Such is the way most houses are
In the Summer-time which poets praise;
  Give me the glow behind the bar
Of a sea-coal fire; or the hickory's blaze;
  And plenty of people upstairs and down
  With smiling faces, and never a frown
  Because there is nobody left in the town.

IN RETURN FOR SOME PRAIRIE BIRDS.

'TIS a pretty fair farm, that of ours in the West;
　And the poultry they raise there, it equals the best;
These hens of the prairie,—I never have seen
A civilised capon more plump or as clean.

'Tis a fine hunting ground the domain we possess,
Some thousand miles off,— sure it cannot be less;
For it took 'em three days, in the mire and the snow,
These birds to bring hither,— the rivers were low.

I have walked over England, and given a look
At all their great houses; but ne'er was a duke,
For all his French pedigree, all his fair crest,
That had such a park as our park in the West.

Gray bird of the wilderness! lucky for you
That you 'scaped the fell shaft of the wandering Sioux!
Then the savage had gorged you, half burnt and half
　　raw,
And tossed your sweet bones a *bonne bouche* to his squaw.

But now you shall grace an Athenian board,
And sparkling libations to you shall be poured;
If Ìowa send game and Ohio send wine,
And Cambridge good company,—may we not dine?

What have they at Windsor we cannot have here?
If we've no royal names, yet we'll have royal cheer:
This only is wanting,—that he were my guest
Whose friendship supplies me with birds from the West.

NATURAL HISTORY OF THE PEACOCK.

THE peacock sits perched on the roof all night,
    And wakes up the farmhouse before 'tis light ;
But his matins they suit not the delicate ear
Of the drowsy damsels, that half in fear
And half in disgust his discord hear.

If the soul's migration from frame to frame
Be truth, tell me now whence the peacock's came ?
Say if it had birth at the musical close
Of a dying hyena,—or if it arose
From a Puritan scold that sang psalms through her nose?

Well : a jackass there was, —but you need not look
For this fable of mine in old Æsop's book—
That one complaint all his life had whined,
How Nature had been either blind or unkind
To give him an aspect so unrefined.

' 'Tis cruel,' he groaned, ' that I cannot escape
From the vile prison-house of this horrible shape :
So gentle a temper as mine to shut in
This figure uncouth and so shaggy a skin,
And then these long ears ! — it's a shame and a sin.'

Good-natured Jove his upbraidings heard,
And changed the vain quadruped into a bird ;
And garnished his plumage with many a spot
Of ineffable hue, such as earth wears not,—
For he dipped him into the rainbow-pot.

So dainty he looked in his gold and green,
That the monarch presented the bird to his queen,
Who, taken with colours,—as most ladies are, —
Had him harnessed straight in her crystal car
Wherein she travels from star to star.

But soon as his thanks the poor dissonant thing
Began to bray when he strove to sing,
' Poor creature !' quoth Jove, ' spite of all my pains,
Your spirit shines out in your donkey strains !
Though plumed bright as Iris, the ass remains.'

So you see, love, that goodness is better than grace ;
For the proverb fails in the peacock's case,
Which says that fine feathers make fine birds too :
This other old adage is far more true,—
They only are handsome that handsomely do.

ALLE SORELLE.

YOU nymphs that blossom in the shade,
　　If every flower that drinks the dew
The symbol be of some fair maid,
　　To what shall I resemble you?

Since not a fragrance nor a bloom,
　　That makes the glory of your fields,
But in its freshness or perfume,
　　Some likeness to your beauty yields.

One to a chaste magnolia's flower,
　　Sole bud upon the virgin tree,
I might compare ; but scarce the power
　　To tell you why belongs to me,

Save that her sunny presence wears
　　The radiant aspect of the South :
Long Summer days and Southern airs
　　Shine in her eyes, play round her mouth.

But you, to one another vowed,
　　Who lead the sacred life, apart
From the vain clamour of the crowd,
　　From the wild tumult of the heart,

In your own groves your emblems grow,
  Walled round with silence everywhere,
And lifted from the world below
  To healthier soil and purer air.

For thou, of eye and soul serene,
  Seem'st, lady whom I most adore!
A mountain laurel, ever green,
  Sprinkling the hills with Springtime o'er:

No matter whether Summer's drought
  A look of withering Winter bring,
Or if December's blast be out,
  Where thou art dwelling, — it is Spring.

Thy sister is that modest, pale,
  And sweetest nursling of the wood,
That men call lily of the vale
  Because it dwells in lowly mood:

Under the laurel shade it grows,
  Nestling itself so close thereby
That, when their blossoms fall, the snows
  Of both together mingled lie:

And both in beauty seem so even,
  That now I worship one, and now
Find in the other half my Heaven,—
  Guess, O my dearest, which art thou?

MUSICA TRIONFANTE.

IN the storm, in the smoke, in the fight, I come
  To bring thee strength with my bugle and drum—
My name is Music,—and when the bell
Rings for the dead man, I rule the knell;
And when the wrecked mariner hears in the blast
The fog-bell sound,—it was I who past.
The poets have told you how I, a young maid,
Came fresh from the gods to the myrtle shade,
And thence by a power divine I stole
To where the waters of Mincius roll;
Then down by Clitumnus and Arno's vale
I wandered, passionate and pale,
Until I found me at sacred Rome,
Where one of the Medici gave me a home.
Leo, great Leo, he worshipped me,
And the Vatican stairs for my foot were free;
And, now I am come to your glorious land,
Give me great welcome with heart and hand.
Remember Beethoven,—I gave him his art—
And Sebastian Bach and superb Mozart:
Join them in my worship; and when the swell
Of their mighty organs hath laid a spell
On every sense, and thy cares are drowned,
Hear the voices of heaven through the men Heaven hath
  crowned.

TO JOSEPHINE * * * * *.

WITH IVY LEAVES.

THIS ivy that hung on the garden-wall,
    In sunlight, in moonlight, in rain, in dew,
Shall glisten to-night in the festive hall,
    And gather fresh beauty and grace from you.

Like a pearl-drop plucked from the deep, to gleam
    On the ivory throne of a lady's wrist,
To-night shall its loveliness lovelier seem
    On the head by whose tresses it shall be kissed.

DIRGE

For one who fell in Battle.

ROOM for a Soldier! lay him in the clover;
 He loved the fields, and they shall be his cover;
Make his mound with hers who called him once her
  lover:
    Where the rain may rain upon it,
    Where the sun may shine upon it,
    Where the lamb hath lain upon it,
    And the bee will dine upon it.

Bear him to no dismal tomb under city churches;
Take him to the fragrant fields, by the silver birches,
Where the whip-poor-will shall mourn, where the oriole
  perches:
    Make his mound with sunshine on it,
    Where the bee will dine upon it,
    Where the lamb hath lain upon it,
    And the rain will rain upon it.

Busy as the bee was he, and his rest should be the clover;
Gentle as the lamb was he, and the fern should be his
  cover;

Fern and rosemary shall grow my soldier's pillow over :
       Where the rain may rain upon it,
       Where the sun may shine upon it,
       Where the lamb hath lain upon it,
       And the bee will dine upon it.

Sunshine in his heart, the rain would come full often
Out of those tender eyes which evermore did soften :
He never *could* look cold till we saw him in his coffin.
       Make his mound with sunshine on it,
       Plant the lordly pine upon it,
       Where the moon may stream upon it,
       And memory shall dream upon it.

' Captain or Colonel,' —whatever invocation
Suit our hymn the best, no matter for thy station, —
On thy grave the rain shall fall from the eyes of a mighty
    nation !
       Long as the sun doth shine upon it
       Shall glow the goodly pine upon it,
       Long as the stars do gleam upon it
       Shall memory come to dream upon it.

PROEM TO A TRANSLATION OF MANZONI'S ODE ON THE DEATH OF NAPOLEON.

(IL CINQUE MAGGIO.)

Inscribed to Mary Russell Mitford.*

I.

READ what the Christian poet saith,
   O lady ! in my faithful rhyme,
Of the great Captain and his death ;
   And venerate, with me, that Faith
Which in the aspiring man of crime,
   Whom gentle goodness must abhor,—
Who carried into every clime
   The fury and the waste of war,—
Some seeds of pardon can discern ;
Yea, from his dying pillow learn
A lesson worthy of the solemn strain
That long as all his triumphs shall remain.

II.

Him and his history of blood,
   Him and the ruin that he made,

---

* This was published in 1854.

By Moskwa's rivulet and Egypt's flood,
　All his bad victories, displayed
On many an arch and boastful pile
That wake the wandering Briton's smile,
　To find no name of England there : *
These can the lenient Muse recall,
And breathe forgiveness over all,
　With a majestic prayer.

III.

Child of his time, the poet speaks
　Such thoughts as to the time belong —
No more his private malice wreaks
　In the small vengeance of a song :
That day of doom,—that bitter day,
When Hate sate sov'ran o'er his lay,
　And bade him, in his burning line,
　To an eternal curse consign
God's universe,—hath passed away.

IV.

For, men who seem to shape their age,
　Yea, fashion history to their will,
And on Fame's perdurable page
　Write their own record, good or ill,—
Even these, if rightly scanned,

* *Par exemple, l'Arc de Triomphe de l'Etoile.*

H

Are but the ivory toys upon the board
  Moving, to lose or win,
By force of mitre, crown or sword, —
  Yet all their little leaps have been
Directed by a wiser hand !

v.

Therefore the gracious Lombard muse, benign
  Interpreter of Rome,
Finds in this Attila one spark divine,
  That hath in heaven its home :
So welcomes him to his eternal rest!
With such high music as befits the blest.

VI.

Not so the grave Etrurian lyre
  Had sounded, in that sterner age
When vengeance thrilled the quivering wire,
When what the poet thought was fire —
  And what he said was rage :
When the great Ghibeline, gloomy and unsparing,
Moved like Fate's shadow, at his girdle wearing
Peter's lent keys, — the while his iron hand
Held Pluto's passport to the sunless land !

VII.

He, to these images of wrong
  Wherewith his unforgiving heart

Peopled the pitiless realm of his dark song—
To Dionysius and his tyrant throng *
  Had added Bonaparte:
And with the rest of that fell brood,—
  Pyrrhus, and Obizzo the fair,
  And the grim Paduan with the raven hair,—
  Had sunk him in that river of despair,
To drink his fill of blood.

VIII.

But He that, in the midst of wrath,
  Remembers mercy still,
Reveals by Calvary a path
  Conducting out of ill,
Into the glad, immortal fields above,
Where His great justice is allayed by Love.
Be this our trust: and may the lofty bard
  Who rules the Latin minstrelsy to-day
Soften within us what is harsh or hard.
    Here calumny should cease—
  Peace for the weary soldier let us pray,
  Since by that lone and lowly death-bed lay
    His cross,—who was the Prince of Peace.

---

* Dante, in the twelfth Canto of the Inferno, describes the tyrants who outraged humanity as plunged in a river of boiling blood, while Centaurs gallop about the stream, shooting them with arrows. Among these sinners he numbers Attila, Dionysius, Obizzo of Este, and Ezzelino the tyrant of Padua.

INSCRIPTION

For an Alms-chest made of Camphor-wood.

THIS fragrant box that breathes of India's balms
    Hath one more fragrance,—for it asketh alms ;
But, though 'tis sweet and blessed to receive,
You know who said, ' It is more blest to give :'
Give, then, receive His blessing ;. and for me
Thy silent boon, sufficient blessing be !

If Ceylon's isle, that bears the bleeding trees,
With any perfume load the Orient breeze ;
If Heber's Muse, by Ceylon as he sailed,
A pleasant odour from the shore inhaled,—
More lives in me ; for underneath my lid
A sweetness as of sacrifice is hid.

Thou gentle almoner, in passing by,
Smell of my wood, and scan me with thine eye :
I, too, from Ceylon bear a spicy breath
That might put warmness in the lungs of death :
A simple chest of scented wood I seem ;
But, oh ! within me lurks a golden beam,—

A beam celestial, and a silver din,
As though *imprisoned angels* played within;
Hushed in my heart, my fragrant secret dwells:
If thou wouldst learn it, Paul of Tarsus tells;
No jangled brass nor tinkling cymbal sound,
For in my bosom Charity is found.

A LESSON FOR EASTER.

From Dante.

CHRISTIANS, be staid; walk wisely and serene:
   Be grave, and shun the flippant speech of those
Who think that *every* wave may wash them clean,—
   That *any* field will serve them for repose.
Be not a feather to each wind that blows:
There is a *Shepherd* and a *Fold* for you:
   Ye have a *Leader*, when your way is rough;
Ye have the Testament, the Old and New,
   And this for your salvation is enough.

MORNING DREAMS.

' Presso al mattin del ver si sogna.'—DANTE.

LOVE, let's be thankful we are past the time
   When griefs are comfortless ; and, though we mourn,
  Feel in our sorrow something now sublime,
And in each tear the sweetness of a kiss.
Weep on and smile then ; for we know in this
   Our immortality,—that nothing dies
Within our hearts, but something new is born ;
  And what is roughly taken from our eyes
Gently comes back in visions of the morn,
When dreams are truest.   Oh, but death is bliss !
   I feel as certain, looking on the face
Of a dead sister, smiling from her shroud,
   That our sweet angel hath but changed her place,
And passed to peace, as when, amid the crowd
   Of the mad city, I feel sure of rest
Beyond the hills, . . . a few hours further west.

TO A 'MAGDALEN.'

A Painting by Guido.

I.

MARY, when thou wert a virgin,
　　Ere the first, the fatal sin
Stole into thy bosom's chamber,
　　Leading six companions in;
Ere those eyes had wept an error,
　　What thy beauty must have been!

II.

Ere those lips had paled their crimson,
　　Quivering with the soul's despair,
Ere the smile they wore had withered
　　In thine agony of prayer,
Or, instead of pearls, the tear-drops
　　Gleamed amid thy streaming hair;

III.

While, in ignorance of evil,
　　Still thy heart serenely dreamed,
And the morning light of girlhood

On thy cheeks' young garden beamed,
　Where the abundant rose was blushing,
　　Not of earth couldst thou have seemed!

IV.

' When thy frailty fell upon thee,
　　Lovely wert thou, even then;
Shame itself could scarce disarm thee
　　Of the charms that vanquished men;
Which of Salem's purest daughters
　　Matched the sullied MAGDALEN?

V.

But thy MASTER's eye beheld thee,
　　Foul and all unworthy heaven;
Pitied, pardoned, purged thy spirit
　　Of its black, pernicious leaven;
Drove the devils from out the temple,
　　All the dark, the guilty seven.*

VI.

Oh, the beauty of repentance!
　　MARY, tenfold fairer now
Art thou with dishevelled tresses,
　　And that anguish on thy brow;
Ah, might every sinful sister
　　Grow in beauty, even as thou!

* ' Mary, from whom were cast *seven* devils.'

TO A YOUNG GIRL DYING:

With a Gift of fresh Palm-leaves.

THIS is Palm-Sunday : mindful of the day,
    I bring palm-branches, found upon my way :
But these will wither; thine shall never die,—
The sacred palms thou bearest to the sky !
Dear little saint, though but a child in years,
Older in wisdom than my gray compeers !
We doubt and tremble,—*we*, with 'bated breath,
Talk of this mystery of life and death :
Thou, strong in faith, art gifted to conceive
Beyond thy years, and teach us to believe.

Then take my palms, triumphal, to thy home,
Gentle white palmer, never more to roam !
Only, sweet sister, give me, ere thou go'st,
Thy benediction,—for my love thou know'st ;
We, too, are pilgrims, travelling towards the shrine :
Pray that our pilgrimage may end like thine !

ST. JAMES'S PARK.

I WATCHED the swans in that proud park,
   Which England's Queen looks out upon;
I sat there till the dewy dark : —
   And every other soul was gone;
   And sitting silent, all alone,
I seemed to hear a spirit say,
   Be calm, the night is : — never moan
For friendships that have passed away.

The swans that vanished from thy sight
   Will come to-morrow, at their hour;   ·
But when thy joys have taken flight,
   To bring them back no prayer hath power.
   'Tis the world's law : and why deplore
A doom that from thy birth was fate?
   True, '*tis* a bitter word, ' No more !'
But look beyond this mortal state.

Believ'st thou in eternal things?
   Thou feelest in thy inmost heart,

Thou art not clay; thy soul hath wings :
And what thou seest is but part.
Make this thy medicine for the smart
Of every day's distress : be dumb :
In each new loss thou truly art
Tasting the power of things to come.

VIRGIL'S EPIGRAPH ON THE PALACE OF AUGUSTUS.*

ALL night long it raineth, but the shows return with
    day,
Jove and Cæsar dividing the world and Rome in their
    sway.

These verses were my making, but another bore the bay.
        So for yourselves, ye robins,
        Ye do not build your nest ;
        So for yourselves, ye little bees,
        Your honey is not pressed ;
        So for yourselves, ye oxen,
        You never drag the plow ;
        So for yourselves, ye woolly flocks,
        Your own fleece doth not grow.

* From the anecdote by Donatus.
    Nocte pluit totâ, redeunt spectacula manè :
      Divisum imperium cum Jove Cæsar habet.

    Hos ego versiculos feci, tulit alter honores.
      Sic vos non vobis nidificatis aves,
      Sic vos non vobis mellificatis apes,
      Sic vos non vobis vellera fertis oves,
      Sic vos non vobis fertis aratra boves.

· PIERI, VALE!

WHAT god it was I cannot say,
　　But one there was, when Jove was king,
Who, wandering by some Grecian bay,
Picked up a vacant shell that lay
　　Bleached on the shore, a dry, unsavoury thing.

Nor is my memory well informed
　　(No Lemprière's at hand to blab)
What tenant had this mansion warmed;
Something with which the Ægean swarmed,
　　Something of lobster-kind, perhaps, or crab.

But he, this cunning child of heaven,
　　Trimmed it according to his wish,
Crossed it with fibres,—three, or seven,
Or, as Pausanias thinks, eleven,—
　　And gave a language to the poor, dead fish.

At once, the house, which, even when filled
　　By its old habitant, was dumb,
Now, as the immortal artist willed,
A little sea-Odèon trilled,
　　And trembled low to the celestial thumb.

Enraptured with his new invention,
    Up soared he to the blissful seat,
And having caught even Jove's attention,
Yea, calmed a family dissension,
    Went serenading through the starry street.

With us, the story's the reverse :
    Our souls are born already strung,
But, 'twixt the cradle and the hearse,
Creeps a change o'er us—for the worse !
    The heart hath music only when 't is young.

For soon there comes a sordid god,
    Who snaps the precious chords of sound,
And leaves the soul an empty pod,
A yellow husk,—a dull, hard clod,—
    A faded shell, in which no voice is found.

Save when some bold, but faltering hand,
    That dares to strike the tyrant, Time,
Tries his first impulse to command,
And, where he loftily had planned,
    Spends the last ebbings of his youth in rhyme.

PARADISI GLORIA.

'O frate mio! ciascuna e cittadina
D'una vera città'——

THERE is a city, builded by no hand,
    And unapproachable by sea or shore ;
And unassailable by any band
    Of storming soldiery for evermore.

There we no longer shall divide our time
    By acts or pleasures,—doing petty things
Of work or warfare, merchandise or rhyme ;
    But we shall sit beside the silver springs

That flow from God's own footstool, and behold
    Sages and martyrs, and those blessed few
Who loved us once and were beloved of old
    To dwell with them and walk with them anew,

In alternations of sublime repose,—
    Musical motion,—the perpetual play
Of every faculty that Heaven bestows
    Through the bright, busy, and eternal day.

THE TEMPLE OF CONCORD AT GIRGENTI.

NOT far from Ætna the Sicilian sun
    Shines on a broken fane whose work is done :
The columns linger, but the hymn is ended ;
The smoke of sacrifice, that once ascended
Staining the sapphire with an earthlier blue,
Is vanished with the crowd from morning's view :
Music and garlands greet no more the day ;
Their gods are gone, and ours alone hath sway.

Such is Time's way with temples : look at thine !
Those changing hairs,—the daily-deepening line !
Mark the slow signs,—then in these things of stone,
Read Agrigentum's history,—and thine own.

ROSLIN CHAPEL.

THY beauty, Roslin, woke a loftier thought—
　　Those friars are gone, but not the truths they taught
The mind that planned thee, and the monks that reared,
Censers, bells, candles — all have disappeared :
But the same spirit hovers round thy walls
That hallows Westminster, pervades St. Paul's,
Or makes the pile that sanctifies the Ouse
A place of pilgrimage for my small muse.

When Scotland's poet led his poet-guest
To thee from Hawthornden's romantic nest,
Thou wast a wreck, and Johnson's learned eye
Read in thy stones but barbarism gone by.
Now from a thousand leagues beyond the sea
Men come to wonder at and study thee,
And maids of English tongue but foreign birth
Kneel on thy flags and kiss thy sacred earth.

And when thy second ruin shall come round
And not one stone be on another found

I

The faith which hung those arches and restored,
Shall still raise temples to the living Lord.
The creed of immortality is thine,   .
Whose life depends not on one mouldering shrine.
Your gods, ye Greeks, died long before your fanes :
Churches may crumble, but Christ's word remains.

MY SUDBURY MISTLETOE.

THIS hallowed stem the Druids once adored,
    And now I wreathe it round my bleeding Lord,
So might my spirit around His image twine,
And find support, as in its oak a vine !

' I am the Vine :'—He said ; Lord, then let me
Be just a tendril clinging to the tree
Where the Jews nailed Thee bodily, to grow
Fruit for all fainting souls that grope below.

May this green hope that in my heart is born
Blossom before another Christmas morn !
Then my weird mistletoe I'll cast away,
And hang up lilies to record the day.

LONDON, CHRISTMAS DAY, MDCCCLXXI.

THE END.

www.ingramcontent.com/pod-product-compliance
Lightning Source LLC
Chambersburg PA
CBHW020758020726
47495CB00008B/2496